H Investigations
Volume One

By Caitlin VanMeter

First Printing: 2017
ISBN 978-0-9983630-3-5

Arctos Media, Inc.
1419 Baker Dr.
Kalamazoo, MI 49048

www.caitlinvanmeter com

Special discounts are available on quantity purchases by corporations, associations, educators, and others. For details, contact the publisher at the above listed address.

Trade bookstores and wholesalers: Please contact Arctos Media, Inc.
Tel: 269.599.0111 or email cliff@arctosmedia.com

Beauty is Only Skin Deep

I still haven't gotten used to sleeping alone. It's been a few hundred years now, and I still wake up with a cold spot on one side of the bed. It's a king-sized bed - something a guy like me needs to be comfortable at six and a half feet tall - but I only use half of it. I've tried to fall asleep in the middle of the bed but I wake up with my arm curled around a pillow and a hand resting in the cold spot.

If I wake up like that there's no point in trying to get back to sleep regardless of the time or the level of sunlight outside. I shake off sleep, looping my legs over the side of the bed, and stumbling to the bathroom.

This morning is no different. I don't even look at the clock before I go to wash my face and peer into the mirror, but there's at least some sun coming in the blinds. I have to say I'm looking pretty good despite my mental state. I'm just glad that the rugged look is back in style. I never fit in with Prince or David Bowie or any of the flamboyant looks of the 80s and 90s. But now that superheroes are plastered in all their beefy goodness on every movie poster of the last few years, my lumberjack-esque jawline and beard are all the rage.

My hand is reaching for a razor to start getting ready for the day when I hear an insistent buzzing. The phone. A constant bug in my ear and in my pocket. But like so many other working men, my phone is work, social life, and financials all rolled into one. I dig around the bed as it continues to buzz; my movements grow frantic as it produces no results. Finally I dig it out from the blankets with thumb and index finger gripping it as light as I can.

The stupid thing is so delicate, I cradle it in my palm as I attempt to slide my fingers over the screen. I've broken every phone I've ever owned within six months of using it, trying to hold onto a few ounces of plastic without crushing it into dust might not seem like a problem for some people but with my strength it happens all too easily. This time I paid extra for the tough outer case, but I still tap the screen with fairy-light touches to scroll through the incoming text messages.

It could only be my favorite brother. Actually Herman is the only brother I am on speaking terms with at the moment. It helps that he is in charge of my website, accepting emails from potential clients and arranging meetings and appointments. Though I actually enjoy talking to him, at least when he's speaking English and not text chat as he is right now. My brain translates his scatterbrained shorthand as I read the series of messages. He can't ever put his thoughts together into one co-herent message, it comes out in parcels, like scattered raindrops.

got some wrk

domestic grab n go

even involves a celeb!

ex of col kingsley wants to meet

needs sm help

right up ur alley

whatcha think?

u there?

Cole Kingsley, linebacker for a rather infamous Motor City team, recently made headlines during the dramatic downward spiral of his marriage. Allegations of domestic violence and a Stepford Wives-esque household of ridiculous expectations and control were at the forefront of the divorce and ensuing lawsuit. That's what my brother meant by domestic. A case involving a husband and wife, or girlfriend and boyfriend, or life partners, or whatever they wanted to call themselves. These are the bulk of my cases.

As for the "*grab n go*": basically the ex wants something from Kingsley that she wasn't able to get through legal means. I either offer him an under the table amount from her to purchase the item semi-legitimately or... well, the name does give it away.

Despite the questionable legality of these kinds of jobs, I've done them before; never with such a high-profile client. The settlement amount was not announced publicly, but I know she has a bundle of cash and a hefty alimony to play with. She could hire a team of lawyers to get the item back, not the scuzzy private investigator with the dubious background that I am. I don't even have an office.

The phone buzzes again, another prod from Herman. His fingers could move across the keyboard of his phone like a ballet dancer across the stage. Mine are more like buffalo stampeding as I clumsily tap out an answer.

where r we meeting?

He responds almost instantly with the address of a neighborhood whole foods store with a small cafe inside, and a meeting time in an hour. I'm not sure how I feel about her chosen location, but I give him the okay and the phone finally falls silent. As it lands with a thump on the crooked bed, I return to my morning ritual in the bathroom.

I step out of my gray apartment building to the sights and sounds of the city in spring. I love Detroit. Something about the wind and the lake appealed to me; the rough and tumble reputation paired with an undercurrent of hope. And it was just far enough away from the family home in New York

City that I could get some relief, without going so far away that they'd come hunt me down.

At the whole foods store I order some coffee from their little cafe. The girl in dreadlocks eyes me up and down with a smirk that sparkles with a lip ring. Is it that I look out of place? I appear young enough to be here but not dressed the part. Mustard stained jeans, my old bomber jacket with the worn out wool at the collar, and a pair of boots built for mountain climbing or bear wrestling and looking as if they have done a bit of both already.

However, turning my coffee cup around I see a small note in Sharpie on the side of the styrofoam. *Call me*, paired with a phone number and a small heart, when she sees me reading it she gives me a wink. Before I can even respond, I see my client waiting patiently out of the corner of my eye. The cashier's gaze follows me as I walk over to the table by the window, I just barely hear a sigh of disappointment as she moves onto the next customer.

Ellen Kingsley has made an attempt to appear inconspicuous, but has only managed to look completely out of place in her chosen meeting spot. She is dressed in a slim blue dress with a cropped jacket, a silk scarf wrapped around her head and large sunglasses over her eyes; in one hand she clutches a Chanel purse. Surrounded by flip flops, yoga pants and college students, the sophisticated air she exudes combats the smell of patchouli coming from behind the counter.

"Ms. Kingsley." I say, offering out a hand for her to shake before I sit down across from her.

She doesn't stand, but she does take my hand, her manicured nails digging into mine for a moment. Her hands are cold. Most women's hands are colder than mine, but these seem extraordinarily so. My investigative mind is working overtime as we sit across from one another.

"Mr. H?" She asks, folding her hands over her purse which is sitting in her lap. "Your website doesn't share much by way of your name. Herman only told me that you were 'the H of H Investigations'."

"H will do fine for our purposes, ma'am." She is a young woman - though everyone is younger than I in one way or another - still in her late twenties, but skittish. I lean back in my chair and keep my hands on my side of the table. I could pass for a linebacker in the right light, and I can almost feel the fear and tension in her frame as she sits. Old fear and tension, weight she has been carrying around for a long time.

She doesn't speak for a moment, reaching into her purse and retrieving a printout of a digital image. A large jersey in a shadowbox frame, red and white, not from any team I recognize, and not belonging to Kingsley either based on the name and the number.

"It's a football jersey." I say bluntly, attempting to provoke a more in-depth analysis from her.

"Yes." She doesn't rise to the bait. "If I tell you where it is kept can you get it for me?"

"Depends. I'm not a thief, Ms. Kingsley. I don't cat-burgle my way into a house and rip things off the walls. Most of the time the stuff I get for people technically belongs to them, at least it can be argued that way in a court of law."

She seems taken aback by my reluctance. Maybe she came to me because she needs a schmuck? I've been one of those before, but not lately. "It is mine, or rather, it was my father's."

Now we're getting somewhere. I'm glad I keep up with the news and various online tabloids. Ellen Kingsley was born Ellen Lear, daughter of Michael "The Lion" Lear, a man far more legendary in sports circles than his son-in-law would ever be. He was a college player turned coach, a man who made millions grooming the finest teams across America. Retired now, but still a legend.

"Well that's good enough for me. Does Cole know you want it?" Her jaw clenches at the mention of his name. I make a mental note of it and my disdain for the man grows with each passing moment.

"Naturally. It was part of the settlement that it be handed over with a large bundle of my possessions that were in the house here in Detroit. However his agent informs me he went on vacation to Buenos Aires before arrangements were made to deliver my things."

"There a particular reason why you can't wait for the court to settle the matter?"

"My father's will states that he wishes to be buried with the jersey." Thin lips and cold fingers make sense now. Not just old fear and tension, but new grief mingled in.

"Sorry to hear that. I didn't know he had passed away."

"He's been suffering for a few years now. It was only a matter of time, and we were glad of the time we were given. I'm just grateful that he saw me get away from my marriage before he passed. It was the one thing he asked me for. But the fact of the matter is, Mr. H, my father's funeral is tomorrow and I want to honor his wishes."

"I just need the address of the house where it's being kept."

Five minutes later we part ways. As I head for a bus stop - I hate driving and always have - my head is turning over the facts. The item itself was bulky, probably a bit conspicuous to take on public transportation, so I shoot a text to Herman again, asking for a ride.

It seems there would be no surprises. The house itself is easy to get to and pretty to look at, a white two-story Victorian. Those Victorians had been wacky but they had an eye for architecture. I head for the back door, reaching an arm over the black metal fence to unlock it. Sure a seven-foot fence is a good deterrent against an average burglar, but I am anything but average.

A door and deadbolt are not much of a barrier either; one smooth rotation of my shoulder takes the door off the hinges and right out of the door frame. It is so quick that it barely damages the surrounding wood. Within fifteen seconds I'm in the house and on the hunt. I feel a twinge of suspicion, as I hear no beeping from the security system. It's not been enabled. The only reason to do so would be if...

"Who the hell are you?"

It's a good thing that I didn't break into the home of a baseball player or a golfer. Cole Kingsley stands before me with a bare fist raised up. His knuckles are bruised; it conveniently corresponds to a few holes I see in the nearby drywall. His other hand clutches a tumbler of amber liquid.

"It's barely noon." I feel obligated to point out.

He narrows his eyes in response to my introductory sentence, and I raise both hands to shoulder height to show that I'm not carrying a weapon. I adopt an easygoing but polite smile, and even give him a small wave.

"I'm H of H Investigations. I'm here as an agent of Ellen Kingsley. I am unarmed and have no intention of causing bodily harm to anyone or damaging any of your personal property. I was hired to retrieve an item that legally belongs to Ms. Kingsley." I recite the words automatically. Years of investigating have taught me that I should always cover my bases. "I was informed you were in Buenos Aires, Mr. Kingsley. Sorry about the door, I will reimburse you for that."

He still doesn't seem to understand what is going on. Too many hits to the head, or just his natural state of being? I know it is a stereotype to accuse football players of being confused lunkheads, John Urschel is a mathematician as well as a player for the Baltimore Ravens. But the dead eyed look from

Cole does nothing to instill faith in me that he has any brain cells.

I let out an exasperated sigh as he drops his glass and runs at me. Why does conversation never work? I brace myself against his tackle, hunching down to lower my center of gravity. In the instant before the strike I hear the roar of a crowd and feel Grecian dirt underneath bare feet, hear the deep-throated guttural sound coming from an adversary's throat. I've fought real beasts before, but somehow men are always more monstrous.

He hits the equivalent of a brick wall with a soft thud, his 300 pound square frame slamming into mine and abruptly stopping. He groans audibly in pain, not used running into someone who doesn't immediately collapse into a puddle of broken bones and squishy organs.

Even without actively using my strength it is still there. My muscles harbor divine (or rather semi-divine) power. The wind is knocked out of Cole in a sudden exhalation of breath, leaving him gasping and crumbling backwards onto the floor.

"Sorry. I did try and explain myself first. You're just lucky I didn't put you in the hospital and out of work. Which I would be more than happy to do. Why don't you have a seat, drink a glass of water, I'm going to grab what I came for and get out of your way."

I grab him under the armpits like a toddler, heaving him up and into a nearby chair, which he collapses into without protest. I head around the corner and see the shadowbox leaning up against a pile of boxes with more dents in them, probably from feet this time. Ellen would be lucky to get anything she owned back in one piece. I pick up the box and walk out the front door. Herman's Prius is waiting out front, the little guy's fingers frantically tapping the steering wheel.

Five hours later and I'm standing in front of Cobo Hall waiting for Ellen as the sun goes down. She drives up in a sporty little foreign number. She dressed down for our second meeting; she almost looks human this time, with her hair down and a leather jacket on. Still classically fashionable, with a confident sway as she walks over to me. The tension is there, behind the sunglasses, but her body language is stronger.

"Let me." I offer, walking towards her car, but she shakes her head, taking the box and sliding it into her backseat. She passes me a thick envelope that I tuck into my pocket.

"Thanks for your help. There's a little extra in there, Herman told me about what happened to Cole."

"Yeah, weird of him not to be in Buenos Aires."

She leans against the door of the car, a small smirk on her lips answering the question I hadn't asked. "There was a small possibility he would be there. I suppose I should have warned you."

"That's why you called me? To take your ex down a peg?"

She slides her sunglasses up to push her hair out of her face, shrugging one shoulder. "I'm not looking for revenge, Mr. H. I just wanted my father's jersey back. Maybe my father wanted some revenge, and I was just doing one last thing for him. I just heard you could handle yourself if it came down to it."

"I was glad to give him a taste of his own medicine."

"I may not possess herculean strength and stamina like some, Mr. H, but I can hit him harder than you can, where it really hurts: his wallet. Cole won't forget me so easily. He'll be paying for every bottle of champagne I drink for the next twenty years." She pauses, small frame taut with brimming energy.

"Listen I…" I rarely stumble over my own words, I've always had some confidence in whatever I saw, but I still look around and tug on my shirt collar like the words need to be pulled from my throat. "If you ever need anything… let me know."

She pauses, suspicion in her gaze. "I can take care of myself."

"But if you ever need anything. Or just want to get away from the lifestyle of the rich and famous and hang out with a bum."

There's no trust there, but some amusement in the crinkle of her eyes. She stands in front of the open door of her car, one foot already resting on the bottom door frame. "You know where the Old Shillelagh is?"

"Of course."

"My father's wake is going to be held there. Tomorrow night, 7pm. There's going to be a lot of sports people there, his old friends from the business, my relatives, so on."

"I'll buy you a drink."

"It's an open bar." She gets in and slams the door.

"Even better."

As she drives off I mosey down the flight of steps leading to the water. The sky is painted with broad strokes of color. That special kind of Michigan pink, with bits of phosphorescent orange and dusty purple at the edges. It smells of dirty water and dead fish, but it looks like a postcard.

Off with Their Heads

My flight lands in JFK at eight o'clock in the morning. As the wheels hit the runway with that thudding, screeching sound, I am still rubbing the remnants of sleep from bleary eyes. Out my window I can see the city skyline of "The Big Apple". Glass and metal and brick piled on top of one another. A city bursting at the seams. I can just barely see the black spire of the company's building off in the distance. Within, my family awaits.

I suppose I should back up a bit. What am I doing in New York? Why am I to see my family after all this time? And where in heck is my ride from the airport?

I was sound asleep when my cell phone rang with an unknown number. Groggy, I picked it up and grunted into the receiver.

"Nice to talk to you too, brother." The voice on the other end was familiar, but my memory banks and the rest of my brain were still rebooting. I just let out another questioning grunt and she answers readily. "It's Virginia, dear."

Virginia, daddy's little girl, my father's favorite child, and his most loyal. She was given every advantage in life, not just supreme intellect, but also stunning beauty. She is always civil, but that doesn't mean much, she's civil to everyone she wants something from. And if she was calling me, then it only meant one thing.

"What does Dad want?" I said, finally able to form a full sentence without feeling like my tongue was three sizes too big for my mouth.

"Always straight to the point. Don't you want to chat a bit, catch up on things?"

"It's four in the morning."

"Sorry, I'm having brunch here in Athens, I forget about that silly time change." Virginia is in charge of the European branch of my father's company. She wines and dines politicians and businessmen all over the continent - or alternatively digs up a nice hefty chunk of blackmail - in order to advance the company's interests overseas. I don't think she's ever spent more than a week or two in the States in the last few hundred years. She also has a flawless memory, so forgetting the time change is nearly impossible to believe.

"Get on with it, what does he want?"

"Olympiad Financial needs you. A specialized investigation needs to take place and you are the only one who can perform it properly." She is only nice when she wants something. But somehow no one catches on and it works every time.

She is the ultimate tactician, a supreme strategist, even more than the brother who actually devoted his life to warfare and the applications thereof.

"I have a job you know."

"Yes, private detective. Quaint." She was growing impatient, which only made me smirk and lean back on the bed.

"Go on."

"Someone in the R&D department in New York is selling company projects. There is a large and very classified project that could be at risk. If it were to be leaked it would be a huge financial loss and might lose us one of our most important partnerships."

"What a tragedy. The multi-trillion dollar corporation will lose a few million dollars and a friend. Isn't it your job to make new friends for the company?"

"Father is prepared to pay you four months worth of your previous salary to come on as a consultant. He contacted me specifically to try and get you to handle this. He's not asking you to come home, Her-"

"I go by H now." I interrupted.

Her voice became sharper, but she maintained her tact and civility. "He's not asking you to come home permanently, *brother*. He simply wants your particular skill set in this particular instance."

Everything I've been working for for the past few years told me to say no. Going back to New York City only encourages my father, and it serves to piss off my stepmother. I also knew, however, that I haven't had too many jobs since spring and here we are in the melty gooey center of July. The savings account is looking mighty slim. By savings account I mean the coffee can with the hole cut in the lid in the kitchen by the way.

Besides, Dad won't be in New York. He hasn't shown his face to anyone in a few decades. No one is entirely certain where he is. He does that sometimes. We call it "going walkabout". He still manages to get in touch with Virginia or my stepmother, the relatives he actually pays, I mean cares about, but other than that he is anywhere or nowhere. Getting the family paycheck without having to actually interact with the family is ideal.

Virginia was waiting me out, a common sales tactic. First person to break the silence is the loser. Thankfully I've always been something of a loser. "Fine, I'll take care of Dad's little problem."

"I'll be sending you an email with the details, your flight for New York City leaves in four hours. You did get a...*complimentary* upgrade to first class." With that, Virginia hung up, leaving me in the dark of my room.

I sent Herman an email when I was in the taxi that I was going to be out of town for a few days. I was tempted to get a ride to the airport in the Prius, but the little guy would have wanted to come along. As it is, he sends me a "*wtf dude, why are you going there?*" with a frowny face emoticon.

Herman is one of the good kids, never in much trouble despite being another of Dad's bastards. When I took off for Detroit he inexplicably followed, saying he also needed a break from the family business. Being stuck in the Olympiad Financial IT department just wasn't the kind of life for Herman. He needed to fly from the nest. Why he chose to play second fiddle to a burnt out detective in Detroit rather than fly off to Paris or Rome or somewhere exciting and temperate is anyone's guess. I never really asked. Everyone has their reasons for leaving the family behind.

That was a little less than six hours ago, though it feels like forever. Heading out of the terminal I spot my ride, so that's one problem down. A thin wisp of a man dressed all in black is holding a sign with "Mr. H" in childish block letters.

He insists on taking my duffel bag even though it is my only piece of luggage.

Olympiad Financial is located in Manhattan, a long drive with plenty of New York City traffic. I hide in the backseat and attempt to catch another brief nap. I don't want to make small talk with the driver, though I'm sure he's a nice enough guy. Now that I'm actually here in New York City, and I can feel the family's looming presence in the distance, there is a knot in the pit of my stomach.

There is something in the eyes of an immortal. A darkness that seems to go down, down, down into them. The skeletons in the closet, the ruthlessness, the disregard for mortal lives. I start to wonder; when other people look into my eyes, do they see that darkness? Am I just like them? That's why I quit Olympiad Financial and tried to quit the family.

I realize as the car zips away that I never did get the driver's name. The entrance to the company is expensive and opulent, but the white marble screams "We're better than you" and makes me acutely aware that I refused to wear a tie. I even find myself tugging at the collar of my business casual shirt as I walk up to the front counter.

After an introduction to the receptionist she goes about making the right phone calls. Pretty, but in a corporate sort of way. Tight knot of hair at the back of her head, expertly manicured fingernails, sitting straight in her chair like she's strapped to it. She smiles at me only with her lips as I wait for someone to escort me.

"Welcome Mr. H. I've heard good things about your skills, hopefully you will be able to help us out with our little problem." The man who comes to meet me is wearing a black suit and tie, square jawed and broad shouldered, very private security, with the haircut and close shave of an ex-military man. He takes me to the first basement level where the security offices are located. The rest of the building is decorated in modern black and white, but the security offices have always been a dingy, concrete gray, too small for the number of staff members it sported. I am shown to a closet-like office with an empty desk. "This is your set-up while you are here. Anything you need will be brought in. A computer is on its way from IT right now, should be here within an hour."

"It's just H. What is your rundown of things? Are you the new head here?" I ask, sitting on the edge of the desk and giving him a closer look.

"Temporarily. The previous head went on an 'extended sabbatical', he called it, taking 8 months off to do something or other. He's family, so he gets the special treatment all the rest of the entitled ones do." Clearly this guy is new, and doesn't know that he is talking to yet another one of "the entitled ones". But I am pretty out of the loop too, because I have no idea what family member had taken over from me as Head of Security once I left.

"Then you know the situation."

"The problem is in R&D. Their head is off in Europe right now working on a manufacturing deal. The team that was left behind have all been working on different pieces of one of our larger and more secret projects. Project Daedalus is a defense project, though there are some civilian applications. A solar-powered drone, lighter in weight than anything else we've built and therefore almost invisible. Add in solar power and you have a drone that can fly almost indefinitely without being detected."

"So someone leaked Daedalus to a rival?"

"No, the good news is that Daedalus is still unknown outside R&D and Security. The first project that was leaked or sold was a minor one, an improved insulation material. Same goes for the more recent project that went missing and then conveniently showed up on Veridian Dynamics' promotion for upcoming projects. That was a minor project too, just some water filtration system."

"So someone is selling off small projects, and you are worried they are just testing the waters for a buyer for Daedalus?"

"Bingo. And we can't find out who the seller is. No one has showed up at work in a new Ferrari and all the camera and keycard data doesn't lead anywhere."

"Perfect. I like a challenge." I hop up off the desk. "I just need a security pass, and I'll get out of your hair."

With a nod the guy walks away. I didn't get his name either. I'm really slipping today. I follow him to his office, thankfully his name is on the door: Bill Goodman. He prints off a temporary badge and laminates it for me. The barcode at the bottom will give me full access to all corners of the building.

Corporate espionage is easy for me. The fact is that a good chunk of employees will end up stealing from the company in one way or another. Most of it is harmless, we've all ended up with a pen from work either accidentally or deliberately.

In R&D the problem is a little more complicated. The employees are scientists, developers, engineers, doctors and basically the smartest people from all around the world. They are also frequently underpaid starting out and have the most expensive student loans to pay back of anyone in the company. M.I.T. isn't free.

Our rivals know this. Clever, anti-social nerds like to feel wanted, and they love having their egos stroked. They are stuck in a basement for most of their careers, and the bigwigs only notice when the technology breaks or doesn't work, and they don't think about all the hard work that goes into making it work seamlessly and smoothly the first time.

The labs are located on basement levels 2 and 3. White and chrome, well-lit with plenty of glass sliding doors opening and closing with a quiet *whoosh,* walking through makes me feel like I'm walking onto a Star Trek set. Machines beep quietly and if anyone does speak they do so in hushed academic voices. The quiet is mingled with the tapping of keys on a keyboard and the scrape of chairs along the cold tile floor.

They start to notice me in phases, glancing up from their work and looking my way, then pretending to get back to work, but aware they are being watched. The Heisenberg uncertainty principle can easily be applied to social situations. "The act of observing changes the nature of the observed."

Finally someone makes eye contact and I reach out a hand to introduce myself. "Hi there, I'm H."

The woman who has the privilege of being my first victim is pretty stereotypical for most of the female scientists I've met these days. Sharp black framed glasses, a messy ponytail, and a rather frumpy over-sized blouse underneath her lab coat. She is pretty though, large doe eyes hidden behind the thick frames and freckles dotted over a pert nose and across high cheekbones.

"Lara Kackias. You said your name was Asch?" She asks, with a hint of an accent. It becomes more Eastern European as we speak further, but her English is impeccable.

"H, like the letter, you know, H, I, J, K, and so on and so forth." I say with a grin, taking a casual lean against the counter she is working on. She swivels on her stool, sliding her glasses up to the top of her head to scrutinize me further. "Nice to meet you Lara. How's your morning going?"

She wants to question why I'm here and what I want, but social etiquette dictates that she respond to my chit chat first. "The morning is going well, Mr. H, thank you for asking."

"It's just H, please." I wink amicably. She doesn't even blush.

"It is a curious name. Like James Bond or an action film star." She relaxes on her stool but she is still bursting with questions. "Are you an actor? Are they filming another commercial perhaps?"

"I'm flattered. No, I'm just a security consultant. I'm here to check up on you guys. And also figure out who is stealing company property and selling it to the competition."

The room falls completely silent. I was well aware that everyone else had been listening intently to my conversation with Lara. The lab is a wide open space and sparse fabric means that voices carry easily.

The silence tells me one thing for sure. Everyone knows that company secrets are being stolen. But do they know by whom?

Ω

If I dealt with one of the egomaniacs upstairs in Sales or Marketing I probably would be more subtle. I would pretend to be a fellow salesman, probably a trainee, new to the world of Olympiad. Salesmen love to share tips and tricks. One "three martini lunch" later and I would know who was skimming from the company and be done with it.

But no one is going to believe that spiel down here in the catacombs. If I pretend to be a salesman they would blow me off, and if I pretend to be a fellow scientist they would see through my limited knowledge. By giving myself away I have established that I know what I'm doing, that I should be respected, and that I mean business. No point in beating around the bush.

Conversation was stilted after that, every sentence chosen carefully, but I persevere. Lara relaxes first, it's not hard to whittle her down with some charm, and slowly the group gets back to work. I'm glad I chose Lara as my first conversation and introduction to the group. She's a tier 3 researcher so she has some seniority, and knows more about what's going on in the company outside of the scientist's cave. Plus, as I said, easy on the eyes.

"Am I a suspect?"

"I wouldn't insult your intelligence by answering that question, Lara."

"Everyone is a suspect, I know. The company wouldn't bring you in otherwise."

I make my way around the room once Lara insists on getting back to her work. While it's true that most of the work going on in here is over my head, I'm not so stupid as to miss someone slacking off. Foot tapping impatiently, the technician's eyes following me around the room even though I never catch him looking this way. He is faking poorly.

"Hi there, how are you doing over here in the corner?"

He alt-tabs away from the screen and spins in his chair to look at me with a friendly but evasive shrug. "H, was it? How did you come by that moniker?"

"My parents graced me with an awkward name. H was just easier." I decide to take a seat next to him, folding my hands in my lap and resting one ankle on the opposite knee.

"Ah, like... Hamish? Homer? Herschel?"

"Something like that." I gaze at him silently for a moment, but with an amiable smile. "I didn't get your name."

"Kevin Soto."

"So Kevin, what's more important than the research and development of fine Olympiad Financial products?"

He flushes with embarrassment, and it occurs to me just how much he looks like one of those red squirrels. Maybe it's the big pointed ears or the small rodent-like face, or the ginger tufts of hair sticking straight up and out in every direction. It is uncanny.

"I'm not here to bust people for slacking off," I assure him as he fishes around for either a desperate apology or an excuse, "I'm a little surprised you would be gutsy enough to do it while I'm in the room, since you know who I am. But unless there's an email with Veridian Dynamics on that other tab, I'm not concerned."

"No, no, it's just… poetry." He sighs, almost wistfully. "I get hit with the writing bug sometimes, I just need to get it out before I explode." He goes on to describe his poetry and the budding artist and desire for creativity in this dreary place, so on and so forth.

Spending time with the lab workers gives me a slightly better idea of what is happening. None of them are showing any telltale signs of sudden extra wealth. New jewelry, nicer shoes, recent trips to the gym or salon. No employee would be obvious in splurging on a several thousand dollar watch, for instance, but he would treat himself to a several hundred dollar watch and some dry cleaning.

I hate to admit it but Lara seems the most likely culprit. She is the most charismatic, she has seniority, and something about her appearance is off. She looks like a dowdy academic but she is charismatic and clever and witty. Is she going out of her way to hide extra money by dressing cheaply during work hours?

I also know that as one of only two women in the lab and the only woman with seniority, she is probably harboring some resentment. Women in science are not treated with the respect they deserve. Never mind that radiation, DNA, and more were discovered by women, and that science fiction was invented by a woman.

In my first lifetime women were seen as ferocious. The Amazons, the Spartan wives, just look at the things my sisters did. Women were fearsome and divine. They still are, don't get me wrong, but they aren't treated that way.

Nothing I know helps just yet but the pieces are certainly swirling in my head. I return to the cupboard-like office and take a seat at the newly installed computer waiting for me. The personnel files aren't that informative either. Lara has an impeccable record as do most of the lab guys. Lara has a lot of recent overtime, but so does everyone else on the Daedalus project.

I wait until after hours and head down to the lab, it's quiet except for the hum of the machines around me. Lara's computer sits by her stool; I access it with the security administrative password, created to override every employee, excepting the CEO himself.

Her company email is clean; discussions of Daedalus are treated with appropriate care for the secretive project. Her personal files are also clean, specs on the project are all password protected. But she has an awful lot of project files.

As a tier 3 researcher, Lara is charged with overseeing progress on multiple projects. Reasonably she should only be juggling 5-6 projects at any point in time. She has files for thirteen active projects. And two of these are from the research center in Chicago. I click a few files and notice that a few of them have been accessed from remote computers. Lara working from home, or taking her show on the road to a competitor?

Before I can download the file information I hear a keycard beep. I slide quickly out of the chair and glance around for a hiding place. I had flicked one set of overhead lights on, but there are large shadows in the corners of the room, and I stand in one of these behind an outcropping of ductwork.

"Did you leave the lights on when you left?" Lara's voice, a bit worried. Her heels click as she walks over to her computer briskly.

"Of course not. Probably Janitorial." This voice is one of the other lab technicians I met today. Ted Fleckenstein. He seemed pretty average, he was one of the least educated guys in the lab, the only one with a lowly Bachelor's degree.

"Hmm, I was sure I logged out of my system too." Lara says, typing away.

"The files?"

"The project is secure, I already shifted a copy to my remote server."

Ted walks up behind her. I can barely see his sneakers from where I am pressed up against the wall. "We need to move on this now that that security guy is snooping."

"We still do not have enough funding." Lara's voice is sharp, almost aggressive. "We just need one more project to sell and we can finish our work. The company will come after us and we need support. Financial and corporate."

"We'll never be able to sell another one now that the company is breathing down our necks."

"Parker will know what to do." Lara logs off her computer and I hear her heels click against the cold tiles as she walks away. Ted's feet linger.

I step out of my hiding place and reach for him. He is turned away from me; I grab his collar and drag him backwards like a dog being pulled away from his food bowl. I release him, but he is now pressed against a table, and I take my place in front of him, towering over his scrawny frame.

"Evening Ted."

"Shi-" He curses and splutters for a few moments, floundering for a good answer.

"You can still save yourself here, Ted. Lara is the mastermind. Who is Parker?"

"P-parker diRossi." He answers instantly, thinking nothing of giving Lara any loyalty at all. "He's our contact at Veridian, a headhunter. He approached Kinsey and John in March to try and recruit them. He told them if they brought a good project along with them they could get big bonuses."

"Then why are they still working here in the lab? I just met them earlier today, working on polymers or some crap like that."

"Lara intervened. She set up a contract with Veridian. Protection from Olympiad in exchange for minor projects. Then they began negotiations for Daedalus."

I fall silent to consider this. Ted begins to slide away and I meet his gaze, stopping him dead. "Come on, you know better than that. Let's take a walk to Security."

He goes in front of me, heading for the elevator, shoulders slumped in utter defeat. Something catches the corner of my eye as Ted punches the button. Down the hall I swear I see something around the corner. I listen hard, but can't hear anything, so I merely step behind Ted into the elevator and select the floor.

Ted is escorted out of the building with a legal document preventing him from contacting his cohorts. He's a coward, so we're likely safe for the moment. When the lab is empty again, I retrace my steps back into the lab.

I peek at John and Kinsey's workstations and emails. They have a group email discussing Daedalus, with two more names attached. Mike Thurman and Dan Stanford. These two are in Chicago, and shouldn't even know about Daedalus. That brings us up to six. Every time I do a bit of digging I come up with more names. How can they be juggling all this and the company knows nothing?

Lara always reminds everyone in every email to keep details quiet. "To protect the company". But it is obviously code about their little arrangement. But why steal company data in the first place? Lara mentioned needing funding. Selling projects and splitting the money among 6 people would mean everyone gets a pittance. Certainly not enough to make it worthwhile. It would barely cover court fees for the ensuing Olympiad lawsuit against them. Veridian might be willing to "protect" them, but only if the assets outweigh the cost.

I catch a few hours of sleep that night and come in extremely early to head back into the lab and collect more data, a flash drive in hand so I can transport everything back to my office. Despite the early hour, I've only been in the room for three minutes when I hear a whoosh behind me.

I turn and see Kevin carrying a box. I glance at the clock, causing my chair to squeak. He sees me and drops it. I hear something in the box rattle and he curses, but doesn't move.

"Morning. Catching up on something?"

"I didn't expect to see you here. Lara said the lab would be empty." He stammers, bending over to pick up his box. "She sent me here to drop off some parts."

"It's six forty-five."

"She uh… well she didn't want to get in trouble. She took a few pieces of the Daedalus prototype home because she was worried about the thief. She kept them in the trunk of her car; she never took them out or anything. But she didn't want you to think she was responsible."

"She told you all of this?" I ask, as he sets the box underneath the counter at Lara's workstation.

"Yeah, she said she could trust me." He's pumped up by this.

I sigh. Kevin isn't part of the circle. He's just a hopeless romantic. "You're a nice guy, Kevin, but hopefully not that naive."

"I know it looks suspicious, but Lara would never do anything against the company. She loves working here. She and John were talking about the company the other day, how excited they are for some funding."

"What?"

"She was on the phone with this guy, Winston Hunt, he's a huge Wall Street financier. I told her usually Olympiad doesn't need help, but she said if she could get outside funding that Olympiad would be more likely to approve her project."

"What was the name of her project?"

"Icarus."

In the end, Kevin will probably lose his job too. It might not be entirely a bad thing though. Poets need a bit of heartbreak to fuel the creative fires.

I don't have much to do until the end of the day, so I wander around Olympiad Financial, checking in on things. I head to the top floor to take a peek in Dad's office. It always has the best view of Manhattan.

There's someone in there when I open the door though. A woman in a pitch black jacket and matching pencil skirt. Her hair is molded into a dark brown bob tinted with just enough grey to make her look distinguished, same with the wrinkles that show up around the edges of her eyes and mouth. It's impossible to tell exactly how old she is. She could be anywhere between a mature 35 to a youthful 55, though the truth is much, much higher. She is standing next to the window, peering out at the New York City skyline, hands folded behind her back. I attempt to leave the room before she notices, but no such luck.

"I had heard you were skulking around the building again."

Slowly I close the door behind us. "Helen, nice to see you. Surprised actually, given your cute little cosmetic company in Buffalo."

"Well Buffalo is… Buffalo. Sometimes a lady needs a look at the city." She says. Her voice is calm, but I can always hear a hint of disgust. She still hates me. "What brings you back to New York?"

"Just one job. I've got people waiting for me in Detroit."

She goes over to the broad ebony desk in the center of the room, gazing down at a picture of herself and my father. I hate that picture. They both look so stiff, like a politician and his wife after a scandal. "We always come back to him in one way or another, don't we?"

"I'm not coming back."

I thought for sure I'd be nursing a few wounds but she lets me go pretty easily and we don't even argue. Lucky day for me. I hole up in my office until evening checking the H Investigations website and texting on my phone. As the lab winds down for the day and everyone packs up I head in. Lara's station is empty.

"Where is she?"

"She cut out early. Wasn't feeling well. She just left 5 minutes ago maybe." One of the technicians says.

I jog out to the employee parking structure. I get there just in time to see Lara's white coat smacking against the back of her legs as she strides purposefully towards a vehicle. I break into a sprint and stop short a few feet behind her.

"Lara, do you know much history?" I say as soon as I've caught my breath, leaning on a nearby car.

She turns to stare at me, her large eyes glassy like a deer in the headlights. "Depends on the history."

"Are you familiar with the story of Daedalus and Icarus?"

"H, that is not history, that is *mythology*."

"Myths have some basis in fact. In all likelihood Daedalus the inventor really did exist."

"And did he build a labyrinth to hold a minotaur?"

"Maybe he built a really good cage for an angry bull."

"So what is the story of Daedalus and Icarus?"

"Well, as you know, Daedalus was an inventor and craftsman. After building a labyrinth for King Minos to hold the monstrous Minotaur, Minos had him and his son locked away. So Daedalus began to build. He crafted a pair of wooden frames and began grafting feathers to them with wax, one by one. He and his son would fly away from Crete.

"They had to be careful. The wax would melt if they got too close to the sun, and the feathers would become wet if they flew too close to the ocean. Daedalus was responsible; he flew the exact right height. But his son continued to fly higher and higher, against his father's warning. He crashed into the ocean. Daedalus could not save him without getting his own wings wet, so Icarus drowned."

"A poor father then." Lara states as I finish the tale.

"You would prefer that he kill himself?"

"Why did he not attempt to catch Icarus as he fell? Why did he not keep Icarus closer? Why not impress harder upon Icarus the danger? Why not attempt to save Icarus, even if it cost him his life as well? The point of escape was freedom for the both of them, not just himself."

"Is that what you want? Freedom for everyone, not just yourself?"

"You know nothing about me, H."

"I know you're the thief. Plus 4 other Olympiad employees, Parker di Rossi at Veridian, and Winston Hunt."

"We only needed to hide until we had enough money. With Winston in the picture we have the investment we need."

"Enough money for what?"

"A company. Icarus Inc. Our future. Our own business where we are not tied to corporate laws, where we can develop and use science as it was meant to be used. Freedom from board rooms and meetings and making the stock market happy."

"Lara, I knew Kevin was naive, but you? You will always be tied to something. If not the corporation, then to your investors, to the government, to your employees, to society. There is no true freedom. We can't even get away from family if we wanted."

She isn't listening. Too busy living her defiant dream. "Are you going to stop me from leaving?"

"You're still on company property. Bill and his team are removing your friends and their computers from the lab right now. Why didn't you warn them? You saw me corner Ted in the lab last night and ran away."

"It will look better on paper if I make a daring escape. I already have a newspaper on standby to break my story tomorrow morning. Who will the people side with? The pretty female scientist or the faceless corporation that mistreated her?"

I'm outplayed, but it doesn't bother me. Lara is right. If she plays up the publicity she might end up getting Icarus off the ground anyway. She's smart. People hate corporations. A little ragtag group of scientists fighting 'the Man' will look great in the news. "Public opinion matters more than funding, especially if this whole things goes to court."

"Then I'm sure you will understand if I go." Her heels smack against the concrete with purpose as she heads up the ramp.

Bill Goodman meets me back in the lobby. "Well, where is she?"

"I dunno. Her car was already gone by the time I got out there. I must have just missed her."

"Her computer was wiped. All the project files are gone, probably with her on a flash drive or something." Bill says, frustrated.

"I say let the lawyers take it from here." I pat his shoulder. "The important part is you rooted out the problem. No more stealing."

It was over, just like that. Too easy. They weren't so well-hidden as they had pretended to be. A little digging and the house of cards comes tumbling down. Why call me in, pay me the big money? Just a play by the company to try and hire me back? I don't even want to think about it. Home is calling me and I've had enough of New York.

Oh Deer

As I hop in a taxi back to JFK, I feel as if a huge weight falls off my shoulders. I'll soon have the company at my back and a fantastic view of Detroit from the first class window seat. I can't wait to take a walk down the Riverwalk and see a proper Michigan sunset. Even I should know better.

My phone starts ringing just as the taxi gets on the bridge. I glance at the caller ID. I don't even know why I answer, but I do. "Hey."

"Please tell me you're still in New York." It is the voice of my sister on the line. Not Virginia this time, but Diane, her words are high-pitched and desperate.

Diane has always been more emotional than my other sisters. She feels things all too acutely. She has more empathy to the world around us than most do. She might dismiss humans, but she cares for every dog headed for the shelter, and every tree slated for the lumber yard. It has caused a few problems in the past of the Greenpeace variety: attacking whaling ships, tying herself to construction equipment in the Amazon, so on and so forth. I can only assume that is what she is calling me about.

"My flight leaves in two hours and I'm currently stuck in traffic." I say with a sigh. "What's wrong?"

"I need you to come upstate, it's an emergency."

"Why me? I am not working for the company anymore."

"This isn't about the company, this is personal." Her voice now contains a hard edge.

"What about your brother, you know, your twin?"

"Researching wind turbines in California, he can't get here in time."

"I don't know how I'm supposed to get up into the ass-end of upstate New York. You do remember that I don't drive, right?"

"You said you were headed to JFK? I can charter a flight directly to Lake Placid within the next ten minutes, I'll pick you up myself. Please say yes, H, I need your help."

How can I say no? Usually I would rather be eaten alive by fire ants than agree to help a sibling of mine, but she rarely asks me for favors. It must be serious. "Yeah, I guess."

"Thank you, I've got to make plans, but thank you, thank you." She hangs up quickly and the driver glances back at me.

"Still need to head to JFK, sir?"

"Yeah, thanks. It'll be to the Olympiad private terminal though. Do you know where it is?"

"Yes sir."

As he drives up to the airport I pull out my phone to send a text to Herman, telling him I'm going to be taking another flight back to Detroit probably tomorrow. Then I pull up a new message to a different number.

i'm going to have to reschedule our date

blowing me off so soon?

not like that. my sister is in a bind and needs my help

i guess it can wait

i'll make it up to you

i will look forward to that

At the terminal a snazzy Olympiad Financial charter plane is waiting for me. How many strings did Diane have to pull with the company to take a jet upstate? I settle into the luxurious comfort of a plane designed to ferry executives to and from New York and destinations unknown and exotic.

Diane doesn't technically work for Olympiad, but is still funded by them The Olympiad Nature Conservation Fund, a non-profit funded by the company, is her pet project, she's the lead executive up in the wilds of upper New York State. Diane used to be more hands on - working as a park ranger - but took over the business side after a previous executive started embezzling conservation funds. He went missing shortly after, I wouldn't know what to presume about his current whereabouts. Hopefully he didn't meet the pointy end of an arrow.

The jet is in the air for less than a hour. It's not even lunch time when we land in Lake Placid Airport. I clamber down the stairs and see Diane waiting for me. She manages to pull off the woodsy professional look really well, her dark hair is pulled back, flowing down her back in a long fish-tail braid. She is wearing a floral blouse and pencil skirt, paired with flip flops.

"Come on, we don't have a lot of time."

We walk briskly to her Jeep, outfitted for off-road travel. She has the top off and she hops in with her usual athletic grace despite the tightness of the skirt. I grab a hold of the side as she whizzes out of the airport.

Olympiad owns quite a bit of the resort town Lake Placid. The family itself owns two separate vacation homes here, one for summer and one for winter. The conservation fund's office is located in North Elba, south of the lake proper, but not by much. The city is surrounded by forest, and protected by national parks.

Back in our day hunting was how you got food. Yes, it was a sport, but it was also essential. And then that sacrifice was honored, by providing offerings to the gods or utilizing every part of the creature. As society grew and hunting became something done for wealth at the expense of animals, my sister's view began to change. The animals she had grown so close to were mistreated and she drew away from her enjoyment of hunting. Shooting wolves from a helicopter with a machine gun? I think that excursion was where she finally flipped the switch. Now she devotes her time and effort to saving as much as she can of the shrinking wilderness.

Diane's hands grip the steering wheel with white knuckles, her lips are pressed into a thin line. I wouldn't say she was a bad driver, just a fearless one. Which scares the bejeezus out of me. How can any human put themselves in 2 tons of metal and plastic, then hurtle themselves down the road at 70 miles an hour? And even though sometimes I hate the thought of living forever, I'm still not ready to go just yet.

I climb down from the Jeep in front of the glass and wood building. It has a log cabin feel but a modern flair, with wide windows and metallic details. We walk under the Olympiad logo to enter the air-conditioned office.

"Do you remember Ceryneia?" She says as soon as we are inside. No one is in the front office, we walk past a few occupied offices on our way to the largest one, jutting out over the edge of a hill, floor-to-ceiling windows making it feel completely surrounded by forest.

"Achaean if I remember correctly. What about it."

"Not the city, but what happened there. You kidnapped my pet, I had to get him back, one of your penance things."

"Yes, I know, I was just being evasive. Also, 'penance things'?"

"Never mind. Point is, he's gone again."

"Well I didn't take him."

"I know. Some scientists did. Grabbed him while he was on a run."

"So the magical deer was running around in the National Park."

This makes her scowl, crossing her arms over her chest and digging her fingers into her shirt sleeve. "I usually keep track of him, but he got away from me. He *is* a wild animal."

"And you can't get him back?"

"Not easily."

"So have the corporate lawyers take care of it. Say he's company property or whatever."

Diane just gives me a cold stare. The company is good at sweeping most of the problems we encounter under the rug. A rumor of immortality, special powers, most of it is handled as crazed conspiracy theories and thorough documentation. I skirt around it by never using a full name and handling most every-thing in cash. No bank account, no social security card. My landlord was desperate to rent a basement unit and I paid him a very hefty deposit. The only thing he asked me before he handed me the keys was "Are you going to cook meth in there?" Once I assured him that no, I wasn't, he was fine with it.

For my other siblings, it isn't so easy. If they want to do anything worthwhile - not be a bum like me - there are a lot of failsafes in place. My father spent a lot of effort and money set-ting up new personas every twenty years or so.

As such, my relatives feel a certain obligation to not blow their cover. For Diane it is even harder. She has always been a free spirit. A huntress. That includes her hind. The hind of Ceryneia, a fancy way of saying deer, but the deer is pretty damn fancy. Golden hooves and horns and a pure white coat so silken and so smooth that it feels like water running between your fingers. The hind is a symbol of purity, and has always been her most precious pet.

"Dad would never let you hear the end of it." I finally say.

"So help me, please." She is begging, which I haven't heard her do in a long time. When Father isn't around and we have to fend for ourselves no one wants to use company resources.

"All right. Do you know where they took him?"

"The Lake Placid Nature Research Center. It's up on the mountain. They tag bears, track breeding populations, record and combat forest fires..."

"I suppose it won't have that much security. Let's wait until it's dark and we'll go get him."

"Thank you H." She flings her arms around me and squeezes tight.

We wait around with growing agitation until nightfall. Diane pops home to change, bringing back a change of clothes and some lunch for me. I am still dressed in khakis and a polo, but she provides me with a pair of dark jeans and a black sweater. She has changed into a pair of those skintight black leggings and a dark t-shirt. Her hair is still braided but she has coiled the braid against the back of her neck so it is no longer whipping around as she turns her head.

As soon as the sun has dipped far enough past the trees we silently get into her Jeep. The sky is purple overhead, the trees are huge black silhouettes, giants standing vigil over our drive. She turns off the headlights as we snake up a road between the trees.

The nature facility is technically open to the public during the day, the front part of it is a nature center where park rangers do demonstrations. A large poster with Smokey the Bear hangs from the front window as if standing guard. Diane drives around to the side entrance which is clearly labeled "Staff Only".

There are a few cars in the parking lot and one or two lights on in the upstairs offices. Diane and I approach the door cautiously.

"I've only been in here once. Kind of a tour for investors type of thing." She says with a sigh, crossing her arms and thinking hard. "There is a lab where they do testing on this floor, it contains cages for any animals they need to bring in. They have one cage that is big enough for him, way at the back, separate from the others. It's meant for bears or mountain lions. They would probably keep him there."

She hands me a mask, a knit cap with holes for eyes and mouth. I'm surprised she thought that far ahead. She shoves one over her own head, and motions for me to open the door. I give it a wiggle to test it. Metal door with keypad, metal frame bolted into concrete. I tighten the muscles in my arm and give the door one, two, three love taps right on the lock with my fist.

The metal buckles, and I shove my hands into the gap between the door and door frame, peeling the door open like the lid on a can of sardines. It makes an awful noise, a popping sound followed by creaking as the metal whines in protest. I can see fear in Diane's eyes as she glances to the lights up in the offices.

I don't hear anything, however, so we enter. I go first, reaching up on tiptoe to turn or unseat every camera we walk past. We speed up as we go, until we have broken into a light jog. I pull back to let Diane lead the way.

We enter a laboratory with whirring computers and one dim overhead light still on. It's quite a striking difference from the sleek chrome and white corporate labs of Olympiad to this government-funded laboratory. I hear rustling and movement from the only occupant in a row of cages along the wall - a raccoon's little beady eyes peer out of the cage and it hisses.

Diane walks by it and shushes it. It falls silent after letting out a weird growling noise, not quite a cat's meow, but similar enough I suppose. My sister leans into the cage and gazes at the animal for a moment. It looks right into her eyes, almost as if it were mesmerized.

"She says he came through here on a stretcher, unconscious." Diane whispers, pulling something from her pocket and squeezing it between the bars of the raccoon's cage. It must have been food of some kind because the raccoon shoves it right into her mouth without another sound and settles back down on the floor of the cage.

I follow behind as she continues through to another lab room. It is completely dark in this lab except for the glow of the parking lot lights between the blinds. I hunt down and flick on a light switch. Diane gasps and hurries forward, jumping over a chair.

There he is, the Ceryneian deer. He truly is magnificent. He is standing up, awake, but perfectly silent. Huge, moon-colored eyes are gazing into Diane's. Diane has reached her arms through the bars of the cage and has cupped one of the deer's ears, stroking it reassuringly.

I walk over to yank off the lock on the cage, then step aside. The deer is a good deal bigger than the local species, he can gaze directly into my eyes, which he does as he steps out of the enclosure.

Diane clicks her tongue, examining every inch of him. "Now we have to erase the evidence. Can you smash up their hard drives?"

"Hang on, I have a better idea." I pull out my phone and make a call. "Herman, it's me. I need a hand."

Diane scowls. "We don't have time for one of his stupid programs."

I silence her with a look. "This team probably can't afford to get all new equipment after I smash it to bits. Just because they caught your deer doesn't mean we should punish their budget."

"Oh. So you abandoned me to flit off to New York and now you need my assistance? Was it the wicked stepmother? Are you buried underground? Are you in a government compound?" Herman's voice penetrates our argument and puts it to an end.

"I'm in Lake Placid with Diane."

"Oh so you went on a hunting trip without me. No, that's okay, I wouldn't have wanted to come."

"Herman, shut up for a second. We had an incident. Can you erase files from the Lake Placid Nature Research Center computers?"

"Course I can. I can access it via your phone if you still have that remote app I downloaded for you."

"Yes sir." I put Herman on speaker and bring up the app so that Herman can log into my phone. I hunt down a cord from one of the desks nearby and plug in my phone to the closest computer. "You're hooked up."

"Super." After a few moments of silence he clears his throat. "What am I erasing?"

I glance at Diane. She considers it, then shrugs. "Do a hard erase and reboot to the last back-up?"

"Let's see… looks like that will be 36 hours ago. Good enough?"

"Yeah, that's perfect."

We wait patiently, Diane doting over her pet. He begins to fidget however, blowing air hard out through his nostrils. Diane tilts her head to the side, before perking up.

"H, listen!"

I raise my head, but I can't hear anything. What I can see, however, spinning against the window blinds, are flashes of blue and red. "Police."

"Probably a silent alarm or someone saw what you did to the door." She says, grabbing a handful of the hind's fur and pulling it towards the door. I yank out the plug on my phone and hang up on Herman, following behind her. As the lights grow brighter I now hear the sirens that Diane and the deer both heard before. They grow louder - then cut out abruptly- and the pounding of feet, slamming doors, and troupe of voices hits us in a wave.

I follow Diane blindly, she seems to know another way out, she pulls the deer along with one hand, pushing doors open with the other. We arrive at another keycard protected door. I squeeze past them in the narrow hallway and give the door a fireman's tackle with my shoulder, opening so hard that it slams into the wall and sends me flying face forward to the ground. I scramble onto my feet and hear Diane cry out behind me.

"H, look out!" Standing in front of me is a very angry security guard with a taser in hand. He fires before I can speak - though if I were standing in front of a guy that looked like me I might shoot first and ask questions later.

It might be important to note here that I'm not completely invulnerable. I can take a bat or a golf club like a champ, but I've never been able to shake off a bullet Terminator-style. 50,000 volts doesn't completely incapacitate me, but it does hurt like a... word I probably shouldn't use here. I reach down and yank the electrodes out, falling down on one knee. The security guards eyes are wide as dinner plates. The point of tasers is you only ever need to use them once, that's why they are designed to be hard to reload. If I was a normal human I would be curled up in a ball with my jaw locked in place.

Instead I drag myself back onto my feet, breathing heavily. "Ouch." I say simply, wiping a bit of blood from where I bit through my lip.

The guard backs up a bit, but I still need to give him a push to get him out of the way. One palm against his chest sends him into the doorway to the left of us, and Diane and I - plus the deer - all rush down the hall. The deer's hooves clatter against the tile floors, making our getaway less than subtle.

The three of us come thundering out of the hallway into the front lobby of the nature center. It's a wide room with tall ceilings. Rows of cases feature Lake Placid wildlife like snakes, frogs, and insects. The front is a long stretch of windows leading to the nature paths and to the parking lot.

Diane digs her keys out of her pocket and thrusts them at me. "Take the Jeep, I'll distract them."

"I can't drive!" I protest as she begins to drag her deer to the front doors.

"The one on the right is the gas, the one on the left is the brake. The big wheel thing in the middle makes it turn. It's 2014, H, figure it out!" She points at the door. "Now open up!"

I break the door as requested and we head down the front steps in a hurry. Voices begin to shout as we are spotted. "How am I supposed to outdrive them?" I ask angrily as Diane pauses at the bottom of the concrete steps. With one graceful movement she jumps up onto the deer's back, one leg on either side, her hands resting on his shoulder blades.

"Don't worry about it. I'll handle them. You just drive until it's quiet again." She guides the deer fluidly, without needing a bridle or reins, and with a click of her tongue they head straight for the gathering group of police pointing their guns at us. Her hair has tumbled out of her braid, she pulls off her mask. Her skin begins to glisten, a divine pearlescence that causes the police pointing guns to hesitate. She is a being of light and perfection, astride a steed of white and gold. Her image flickers, she appears to expand in size until the hind is a dozen feet tall and she is just as tall upon its back, towering over the police in front of her.

I make a break for the car as the cops falter. I slide in, turn the key. Behind me I hear thumping and the sound of breaking metal and glass. I don't turn my head, focusing forward. The road in front of me leads into the woods, I turn off the headlights and drive forward.

My night vision is not bad, but I still have to swerve every time a tree seemingly appears out of nowhere on the dark road ahead. I drive until I can no longer hear the sirens, and the sounds of the forest at night cocoon me and soothe my nerves. I pull off into a deserted campground and park in the back. In this open area the moon illuminates my surroundings and I don't feel quite as scared anymore. Even a guy like me can feel fear. Maybe more than you might expect. It's a loss of control, to trust the world not to kill you. What good are all my glorious muscles if I can't control my own destiny?

I hear a soft padding noise, like socked feet on a wood floor. Out of the woods to my left comes Diane atop her nontraditional steed. They are back to normal size, but Diane still shimmers with an otherworldly light. Her eyes shine black with golden stars, like the heavens resting in her gaze. The moonlight bounces off the deer's white coat, giving him an ethereal glow. In her right hand is a golden bow, which bursts into stardust as she dismounts, each speck flitting away like a cloud of fireflies into the night sky. She slowly fades back into a more human form as she walks over my way. By the time we meet face to face again she is gathering her thick wavy locks and tying it in a knot away from her face.

"You fired arrows at the Lake Placid Police?" I ask incredulously, removing my own mask and depositing the keys to the Jeep in her open palm.

"Only one or two, and only at their vehicles. A couple of flat tires never hurt anyone."

"You realize that you've made a bigger mess than if you had just asked Dad for help."

She pauses, having turned back to pet the deer again. She doesn't look my way however. "I handled this myself. And I can clean up the mess myself. A sizable donation to the Nature Center and to the Lake Placid Police Department will take care of the damages. I get along very well with both of them."

"And what about him? He'll still be wandering the forests."

"Adam is coming to get him." Her voice falters as she resumes stroking the deer's fur. "I'm having him sent away, for his own safety. And mine. There's a protected space up in Canada where he'll have a bit more freedom."

"You're not going with him."

"I can't. I have responsibilities here. Not everyone can hide away from the family whenever they please." She spits, finally looking at me.

"Artem-" I start, reaching out to take her hand. She shakes her head, her face softening, her eyebrows curve down in an unspoken apology.

"Thank you for your help, H."

I reach over and wrap an arm around her shoulder, giving her a sideways hug. "I'm sure he'll be happier outside of a cage anyway."

She sniffs, covering her eyes with one hand. I release her from my hug, but keep a hand on her shoulder. No goddess wants to be seen crying. After a final pat from Diane, the deer bounds away into the trees, and she climbs into the driver's seat.

"Come on, time for you to go home." She says, voice thick. I slide in next to her, but my eyes follow the reflection of the white fur among the trees until it finally vanishes from sight.

The Other White Meat

"And here I thought we were going to have a nice dinner out without talking about work." I pick up my frosty beer and take a swig.

My favorite pair of kelly green eyes glances at me over her own wine glass. Ellen sets it down and shrugs one shoulder. "I *am* enjoying dinner. But I promised Janice that I would ask about her son."

We're in the Old Shillelagh, Detroit's oldest and best traditional Irish pub. It feels like a dive bar in the heart of the city, it's just clean enough to attract the upper middle class as well as working folk. The important thing is they serve great food and great beer. And it is very much a neutral place to meet with people. There's no pressure in a pub to act a certain way or eat a certain thing. We have half-empty baskets of hot wings and chili cheese fries and we're both wearing jeans and sneakers.

"All right, so tell me what's going on."

She shifts in her seat, resting one elbow on the table in order to sip from her straw. I like seeing her like this. She's dressed down, but her hair and make-up are still expertly applied and styled. Every time we meet she looks a bit different than the last time. A bit better, a bit healthier, a bit happier.

"Janice's son Brandon is in a bit of trouble. He got cut off by her husband a few months ago because he was burning through his monthly stipend and begging for money. He's about to flunk out of U of M, and when Stan found out that he had sold the BMW that was his graduation present and *that* money was gone too, he said enough was enough. Shortly after that happened, Brandon ended up in the hospital."

"How?"

"He claims he was carjacked. Janice let him borrow her car to go back and forth from Ann Arbor on the weekends."

"So another expensive vehicle in the wind."

"Correct."

"Does she suspect drugs?"

"No, she could handle that. She and her husband founded a few rehab facilities. They are... familiar with that issue. This is something else, which is why she needs outside help."

I heave a deliberately dramatic sigh. "I can see I am nothing but a puppet to you rich folks, toyed with until you have need of me. You'll let me buy you wine and hot wings just to keep up the charade."

She is fighting down a smile; she picks up her wine glass again, presumably to hide her amusement a bit more. "Are you actually buying tonight?"

"I had considered it."

"Are you going to take the job?"

"Was there any doubt that I wasn't? She doesn't think she's getting some family and friend's rate, does she?"

"No, I made sure she knew you were very expensive but worth every penny."

"Aw, you do like me." I propped my elbow up on the table and reached over to pluck a wing from her basket.

She reaches over to brush her hand over my knuckles and smiles reservedly. "I have enough money and enough free time to spend time with who I want. And I want to spend time with you."

"That's possibly the most romantic thing you've said to me ever."

"Don't push it, H." She says, leaning back in her seat again. "When can you start? I have to call Janice and set up the meeting."

"At least give me some time to digest. Then you can tell Janice I'll take care of her bratty kid."

"I'll be sure to use those exact words."

We finish up dinner and I walk her out to her car. The wind coming from the river is frigid cold and we skirt around patches of ice. It hasn't snowed yet but it will be any day now. I hold the door open for her, leaning down into her open window. She looks up at me with a smirk. "Are you sure you don't want me to drive you back to your apartment?"

"Nah, I'll take the bus. It's clear on the opposite end of town from you." I lean in when she does for the kiss, brief but meaningful all the same. "Dinner next week?"

"Same time, same place, same pretty face." She says with a wink and drives off.

There's something there that is hard to describe. I'm comfortable with her, like lounging on a worn-out sofa in flannel pajamas with a dog on my lap kind of comfortable. She hasn't been over to my place, I haven't been over to hers. We go out. Mostly to the Old Shillelagh, or to a movie, or just down to the waterfront. She loves Detroit just as much as I do. We talk about the Red Wings, the weather, the road construction, that statue of RoboCop someone decided to build. Other times we sit quietly and just enjoy the world around us. We don't talk politics, or emotions, or religion. It's not forbidden, but we just don't.

The next morning I'm sitting in Starbucks across from a bleach-blond woman in heavy mascara drinking a chocolate-coffee-ice-cream monstrosity.

"I called his roommate today, he's not even at school. He's only a sophomore you know, he has his whole life ahead of him, I just don't understand what he's doing."

"So where would he be if not at school?"

"I don't know. On the weekends he says he goes into the city for clubbing, but he hardly ever comes back drunk. And I just don't believe it."

"What do you suspect?"

"Personally... I think it might be the casino. Gambling. His father doesn't think so, but I have found poker chips and parking tickets in his pants pockets."

"Well I will take a look into it. What do you want exactly? I'll be honest here, he's not going to change his mind if I beat him up, and I don't think you want that."

"No, no! Not that. I just... he's in trouble. Whoever beat him up and stole my car, whoever wants to hurt him, I want you to find those people, and make them leave Brandon alone. If he owes them money, we can pay it. If you can keep them from beating him up or worse, killing him, then I can talk to him, show him that he has a great future, that he doesn't need to do whatever he is doing, he can have a meaningful life." She says.

"So about your husband."

"Don't worry about it. He's on an 'extended business trip' with his new secretary. I have money to pay you for your services, Mr. H, and funds to pay off whoever he owes."

"It's just H, really." I say with a nod as I get up. "I'll track him down. I'll see what I can do. I can't make any promises."

"I understand. I've tried normal paths, therapy, tough love, an intervention, nothing has worked. I just want him safe."

Greektown has always felt a bit like the old, darker Detroit. Not quite as clean and shiny, not quite as flashy and new. It looks like a casino from the seventies, floor to ceiling mirrors line whole walls and the carpeting is designed to hide stains in the worst way. It feels like a seedy sort of place. Fat guys smoking cigars in a corner booth while a cocktail waitress serves them cheap champagne kind of seedy. Detroit has been slowly rebuilding from the ground up and redoing their image, but Greektown hasn't gotten the same facelift just yet.

I know a bunch of guys in Greektown security, and one of them owes me a favor. I give him a call. "Hey Len, long time no see, mind if I come up and visit you?"

With his permission I head into the security office. Lenny looks displeased that I'm risking his job like this. "You couldn't just ask for some free poker chips or something?"

"I don't gamble. But I'm looking for someone who does." I pull out my phone and pull up the image of Brandon that Janice had sent to me. "Do you have that facial recognition stuff?"

"This is Detroit dude. We're lucky we have as many cameras as we do. They don't spring for that stuff here."

"Then I need to plug my phone into your computer."

Herman does his remote thing within a few seconds. Lenny is not looking any happier. If his bosses find out what I'm doing, he would be fired instantly. Though what I did to deserve the favor saved his job a year or so ago. He can't really fight me on this.

"Found him. He's here right now, also looks like there is some archive data of him… going back to the beginning of the year. 72 instances and counting of his face on camera."

"Lenny, one more favor and we're even, I'll never bother you again."

"What?"

"Kick him out and put him on your banned list."

"I gotta have a reason to kick out a customer, and a damn good reason to ban them for life."

"Make something up. Drugs, harassing waitresses, cheating, whatever you can think of."

Lenny grumbles under his breath and then nods. "Fine, he's out."

I stand outside the front doors, under the overpass from the People Mover, as Lenny and one of his team come out, dragging the kid between their arms. It's quite a struggle as he tries to free himself from their grip, his voice carries through the area, not that it's loud, but high-pitched, whiny. "I didn't touch her, I swear it! She's lying! I never would have, I just wanna play, guys come on, I can pay, it's fine! I'll tip her, I promise."

They are stone-faced, releasing him on the front step. "If you enter the premises of Greektown Casino again in your lifetime, the police will be called and you will be arrested." Lenny says flatly. "Your business is no longer welcome here."

Brandon stands there and watches them head back inside, incredulous. He is a big kid, but not in the same way I am. His gut pours over the front of his jeans and is just barely covered by the Red Wings jersey he is wearing as a shirt. He's barely up to my chin, probably five six or five seven if he is lucky. He yanks up his pants every few minutes, peering through a pair of wire-frame glasses with little beady eyes. His cheeks sag, giving him the look of an old English bulldog, especially when he starts panting and leaning forward after the exertion of trying to fight off the security team.

"Brandon Farmer?" I walk forward.

He looks up at me, his entire face going from indignant to terrified in a moment. "Shit, shit, I'm sorry man, I was gonna make a payment, I almost had enough, then those a-holes kicked me out. I swear to god, tell Fakhoury I can make a payment tomorrow, I promise."

"I guess I should be glad it wasn't Russian." I say with a roll of my eyes.

"What? What the hell are you talking about?"

"Don't worry about it. I'm not here to break your knee-caps or whatever."

"Then who are you?"

"I'm H. Your mother hired me to track you down."

"Christ. My mom is such a bitch-"

"Hey." I cut him off and wave a hand at him threateningly. "Your mother isn't stupid. She knows you're in trouble. Do you think you can keep selling your parents' stuff and no one will figure out what you need it for? This Fakhoury guy, who is he?"

"She actually." He grumbles, shifting around. "She's really freaking hot too. But scary."

"And she is the one who carjacked you?" He doesn't answer. He thinks he's the smartest person in the room. I roll my eyes and grab his sleeve. "Listen, idiot. I'm here to save you from yourself. Where is Fakhoury?"

"I don't know." He grimaces. "I only met her once at some crappy bar."

"Is Fakhoury the only name you have?" I ask.

"Her brother, he's the one who..." He falls silent, glancing from side to side. He's been scared for sure, but even that wasn't enough to keep him from continuing to gamble.

"What's her brother's name?"

He doesn't answer. I could force him to answer but instead I switch tactics. "Where did you get the money you were gambling with today? You're supposed to be cut off."

"Mom gave me her credit card so I could buy a train ticket on the Amtrak to come home and in case I needed groceries." He mumbles, shoving his hands in his pockets.

"How much did you rack up on it since she gave it to you?"

"Dunno. Couple thousand." He shrugs one shoulder as if it means nothing. A thousand dollars to him is barely enough to cover expenses for a week, let alone a full month. Reminds me of the senator who said that after taxes he "only" makes two hundred thousand dollars, and how is anyone supposed to live and feed a family on that paltry sum?

"Take me to the bar where you last met with Fakhoury." I order, and when he starts to get squirrely I stare him down until he complies.

"Fine, where's your car?" He asks, glancing around.

"I don't own one. Either it's close enough to walk or we can take the bus."

"You live in Detroit and you don't own a car?" He says indignantly.

"Nope, I sure don't."

He groans, shifting around, until eventually he gives up the address. It's not that far, and would have been a nice walk, if not for the panting, whining man-child on my left. Every step yields a grunt like he's lobbing a tennis ball over the net. We walk a few blocks and he plops himself down on a bench and glares at me.

"Come on Brandon, giving up already? A walk is good for you."

"What's your deal man? I could give you the address and you could leave me alone."

"No, you have to come with me. I want you to see what happens when you get involved in this."

"You think you can scare me straight?" Brandon scowled.

"I think you're beyond that. If you can get 'carjacked' and beat up and thrown in the hospital without thinking about getting help, then you can't be scared. I don't want to scare you; I just want to do what your mom is paying me to do. She wants to pay out your debt. You'll be lucky if you don't end up in this exact same spot a year from now. What happens when your mother gives up on you? Your father already has, from what I hear." He falls silent, sullenly staring straight ahead. I let him stew for a minute. "What's the name of the bar?" I say finally.

He points up the road. "It's the Iris, right down there."

"Sit tight. I'll go drum up some information." I leave him on the bench and walk up the road to the bar. It was a small place, unassuming. I look up at the sign, then the windows, which are coated in grime. Before I even get a chance to enter however, my nose is caressed with a warm, spiced aroma. I turn in place, my stomach waking up and grumbling.

Just across the street from the Iris is a little white shack. Some outside seating and a few rickety tables indoors. The sign over the front door is written in Lebanese and English. *Schawarma Chicken or Beef; Made Fresh; Falafel, Hummus, and More!*

I jog across the street and step inside. Within the small space, probably only 16 x 16 feet total, the smell seems to amplify. I order a beef combo, and watch them stuff a styrofoam container with rice, then the beef, a spoonful of hummus, half a pita, and two round falafel. The lid will barely stay closed as the young lady behind the counter hands it over along with plastic wrapped utensils.

"*Shukran jazilan.*" I accept the container and thank her. She seems a bit startled to hear me say it in Arabic, though my accent is atrocious so maybe I just insulted her accidentally. "Sorry, it's been a long time since I used that."

She lets out a small, contained laugh. She is beautiful, with wide brown eyes and dark curly hair. She looks at me and I am reminded of Egyptians from ancient times, her soft eyes are rimmed with dark make-up and she seems wise beyond her youth.

"I appreciate the effort." She says.

"It smells delicious." I crack open the Styrofoam with a pleased sigh. "I didn't even realize you guys were here."

"We get that a lot. " She leans against the counter.

I hopped up on the slightly rickety chair and dug into the meal. I hadn't realized how hungry I was until I smelled food. "Do you know anything about the Iris?"

"Me and my brothers go there after work sometimes. It's a dump but its cheap."

I reach a hand over the counter towards her. "I'm H."

"Shahla Fakhoury." She shakes my hand.

"Ah. That explains why you are so successful." I say, continuing to eat.

"What do you mean?"

"Using this little place to launder money is pretty clever. What are you importing? Heroin? Is it racist to assume you're bringing in heroin?"

She doesn't answer. I'm assuming that means yes. She leans away from the counter and crosses her arms over her chest. "I have no idea what you're talking about."

"You're right. Only legitimate businesswomen loan out money to stupid college kids in order to weasel unlimited interest out of them."

I can hear her tapping her foot in the ensuing silence. I continue eating because frankly, the food is really good. "You aren't the police. And you have no evidence."

"I have a wimp who will probably point the finger at you if I can scare him enough."

"Then I guess the question becomes who is more frightening, you or I?"

"His parents would like to pay his debt to you with no police involvement, that's why I'm here. They have no intention of pressing charges but they'd like their son to keep all his fingers. If I can get the total sum he owes you then you can make a bit of money on the interest and everyone goes home happy."

"He disrespected me. Perhaps I do not want his parents' money?"

I snap the lid on the container shut, it is still about half-full, tucking the plastic fork into my pocket. Out of my other pocket I pull out a card. "I'm not interested in negotiations. You calculate the full sum, plus interest and whatever fees you need to charge, and my clients will arrange for payment. Call me when you have the number."

She accepts the card, flipping it around in her fingers. "You are a private investigator?"

From the back room emerges a tall man in a long jacket. He doesn't look like an employee, he's not dressed to work in a kitchen. He moves somewhat menacingly. We're about the same height, our shoulders are the same width, we both have handsomely carved jaws and large, intimidating hands. Outwardly it would appear we are evenly matched in the strength department. He comes around the side of the counter, flipping it up and then letting it slam down behind him with a loud thunk.

I set down my food at the other end of the counter. "I am."

"Fully licensed?"

"Licensed enough."

"So you don't work with the police."

"Not generally."

"Apologies, Mr. H, this is my brother." She motions to the man beside her. The man is much older than her, I would have guessed father or uncle rather than brother. Also, there seems to be a difference in appearance that would indicate they are not related. He is blond, for starters, with pale skin and a general lack of facial hair. I would peg him as a surfer long before I would give him the last name "Fakhoury".

"Pleased to meet you."

"Problem, Shahla?" He says casually, sliding his hands out of his pocket. He's surprisingly unarmed, but I have been doing this long enough to see the fabric bunch under his armpit, indicating a small pistol or revolver housed in a shoulder holster. He also has a blade tucked into his ankle, almost invisible unless you know what to look for.

"Lock the door, Jack." She says.

He obeys, walking over to the front door and pulling the deadbolt across the lock with a deafening click. I widen my stance slightly, bracing my heels against the floor.

"I don't appreciate disrespect." Shahla hasn't moved from her place at the counter. "The fat pig came to one of Jack's games. He's very protective of his poker games, you know. Your little piggy was a poor gambler and a sore loser. He threw a fit, knocked over tables, caused quite a bit of damage to Jack's studio."

"And you couldn't have him arrested for the damage because I'm sure this 'game' wasn't legal."

She rolls her eyes. Jack seems to take this as a message, and he charges. I let him come at me, tucking my hands into my pockets. I duck down as he swings his hand out, using my momentum to swing him around into the wall. I pull out the plastic fork and slam it into the palm of his hand. It isn't sturdy enough to withstand that level of force, it shatters and drives shards of plastic into his skin, good enough. I grab his other hand and twist until I hear the crack. As he falls forward I bring my knee up, sending it into his face. He flies backwards, hitting the ground and laying flat on his back in the starfish position.

I turn back to Shahla. The butt of a shotgun is nestled up against her shoulder, the other end is pointing at me. I freeze, staring her down.

"Are you ex-military?" She demands.

"Sort of." I say, wiping sweat off my forehead. My sleeve comes away tinted with red, but it isn't mine. "Is he really your brother?"

"Sort of." She says curtly, adjusting the gun.

I nudge Jack with one toe, he whimpers. "Spiral arm fracture, that'll be multiple surgeries and probably a titanium rod installed, not to mention months of physical therapy. Broken nose, that'll be some cosmetic surgery if sister Shahla will spring for it, I probably loosened a few teeth too, maybe needs his jaw wired shut and probably some crowns so probably some dental surgery after all that too. The longer he sits here the less you know about any internal bleeding or organ damage."

She glances down to him, then back to me, her mouth pressed into a thin line. "Brandon's borrowing sum was 75,000. 50% interest. He owes me 112,500."

"Minus the costs of the two vehicles that you've already taken. Street value of the Beemer is what… 25, 26 to sell it off for parts? 20 if you painted up a pretty title and sold it to someone who didn't ask too many questions. Mom's car was an Audi, so that's 25ish for parts. Let's call it an even 50 taken off the principal, not the interest, so that means he owes you 37 and a half for the remaining interest. Let's add on a sum for your brother's hospital bill as a courtesy fee, shall we? He'll pay 50 even, not a penny more, and once I bring you the money you stay away from him."

She does the calculations in her head quickly, and then nods. I walk to the door and undo the deadbolt, while she ducks under the counter and bends down over Jack. I turn, and she raises the gun again. I point to my styrofoam container, and she slowly follows me with the shotgun until I pick it up.

"Thanks for the meal." I smile at her genially and head out of the place, back down to the bench where Brandon is sitting and texting on his phone.

"I hope you're calling your mom to come pick you up." I say as I sit down next to him.

"What? No, I'm not going back there."

"That's too bad. Guess you and I are going to sit here until she shows up."

"Come on dude, there's a game across town, I can get in and play just a few hands." He says in exasperation.

"With what, your good looks?"

"What's that on your jacket? And face?" He suddenly asks, finally noticing the blood.

"And on my favorite pair of jeans too." I say, pointing to the knee of my jeans, soaked with a dark brown patch from Jack's nose.

"That's blood, isn't it?"

"Ding ding ding. First guess. I found Fakhoury."

"You did? Did you beat her up?"

"No. She's half my size. We negotiated."

"So how did you get so bloody then?"

"Her supposed brother got caught up in the negotiations. I'm assuming that Jack guy is who 'carjacked' you?"

"Oh, shit. You fought him?"

Eventually Janice shows up and ushers Brandon into the car reluctantly. I don't give her too many details except advising her to keep Brandon at home for a bit for his own sake. Brandon cusses under his breath at me for that as they drive off.

Later that evening I pop open the leftover food back at my place. It's dark when my phone begins to buzz insistently. I answer it after swallowing my mouthful of beef. "H Investigations, this is he."

"I appreciate that you called me a businesswoman, H."
It is Shahla's voice over the speaker. "Could you agree to meet?
Brandon just tried to get into one of my games and well... I
think he needs someone to come pick him up. Before one of my
brothers ejects him."

She gives me an address and tells me to meet in an hour.
I barely catch the last bus to the location, which turns out to be
a boarded up storefront. I walk around to the back parking lot,
and see two black vehicles. It is very dark, I can barely make
out a few shadowed figures.

"Mr. H, I presume." The voice is male. Two tall figures
flank a more petite one. I can't see any faces.

"No, it's just H."

"H, thanks for seeing me. I figured your client would
want you to come and get him. Did you call her?" My eyes ad-
just to the darkness. Shahla is wearing a full head scarf, though
it could easily be against the cold as it could be religious,
pinned in place with a glittering butterfly pin near her ear.

"Where is he?" I say, a soft sigh of exasperation leaving my
lips. "I will bill his mother another few hours work for this plus
the cost of the taxi."

"Take care of him." Shahla's tone doesn't make it seem
like this will be the good kind of 'take care of him', where they
just give me what I ask for and I go home without bruises.

Did I know this was a trap? Yes, I had my suspicions, confirmed after a brief text message. I hate being right. The man to her right flings his arm back to reveal a long thin shadow. The golf club comes at me with force, I turn my body to brace it. The man, who appears hispanic in the light from the back door, is the one to cry out in pain, when the club bounces off my shoulder and goes flying, clattering to the ground somewhere behind the cars.

Shahla is dead silent and wide-eyed upon seeing this, but the other reacts as though it were a fluke, coming at me. He has a blade, long and thin, single edged, likely some kind of chef's knife. His arms are shorter than mine though, his reach even with the blade is shorter than mine by about three inches. I reach out with a quick jab, my hand wrapping around his throat. I carry my weight forward, using the momentum to slam him into the ground. I'm holding back, every muscle is primed, only delivering just the right number of force for mortal bones. My palm could flatten his windpipe, crush his larynx, maybe tear his jugular if I hit the wrong angle. As it is, the wind is knocked out of him, and he lays very still. The point of his knife has nicked my chest, it's bleeding, but sluggishly. It'll be gone in a couple of hours.

Shahla stands still, silent. I turn to her, shaking my head in a very disappointed manner. "How many guys of yours am I going to send to the hospital? You want me to shut you down?

I just wanted to do business here. You said you were a businesswoman."

"No, I said I appreciated you calling me one." She says, her voice thick, eyes flickering back and forth to her men. "How could you fight like this? Luis was a Navy SEAL, I didn't even see you move."

"I'm better than a Navy SEAL."

"You're not human." She says. "You.... what are you? *Marid*?"

I chuckle. "You're old-fashioned dear. I haven't heard that word in a long time. Are we done? You probably want to call an ambulance. Oh, and these guys aren't going on Brandon's bill."

She glances around, pulls out her cell, and types something into it. "Very well. We're done. The money transfer has been completed, Brandon's bill paid."

"And me? You gonna call this vendetta or should I start purchasing bulk Hanes?" I say, tugging at my torn shirt, blood seeping into the cotton.

"There will be no vengeance on my end, so long as no reports are made by you or anyone associated with you."

"And what, have you put me away for assault cause it's my word against yours? Nah, I don't really fancy jail time. Can't afford a good lawyer."

She nods, and helps the two men, who are barely conscious, into the back of her large black SUV. She leaves the other car there as she drives off, I step back.

"Holy shit man." Brandon appears from behind a dumpster, eyes wide. I did forget to mention that I called him down here to be my ride home, didn't I? A text to confirm he was safe, and then ordering him down to the address but quietly, telling him to hide and stay hidden no matter what.

"I know I said I wouldn't be scaring you straight, but I changed my mind." I say, wrapping an arm around his shoulders and squeezing just a bit too tight.

"Hey! Hey, man, you don't have to tell me twice." He scrunches up to sidestep away from me, shoving his hands in his pockets.

"You might be clear with Fakhoury but you aren't clear with me or with your mother. You owe her huge now, you realize that? You can't pay her back with winnings."

"I was on such a hot streak."

"Gambler's fallacy, Brandon, you need to look it up. Do some reading. If you're lucky it'll sink in and you might graduate from college without costing your family another hundred grand. Money matters to some people Brandon."

We drive back quietly, Brandon seems lost in thought. As we pull up to my apartment complex, he sighs. "I love my mom you know."

"You could show it. Stop being a fuckwit. Study. Do something. And please, get some help."

He grips the steering wheel, swallowing. "They'd have tried to do that to me, wouldn't they?"

"She wouldn't have killed you. You're no good to her dead. But I've seen worse things than death."

"How edgy sounding. Seriously, are you a SEAL or something like she said? Ranger, maybe?"

"I was a soldier once, but nothing fancy. I've just picked up a few things here and there."

"Right. Well. Thanks anyway. I guess I'm in the clear."

"Not unless you do what she says." I say, my voice biting.

"Yeah."

I watch him drive off. It's not easy dealing with kids. I have a brief pang. Old, forgotten grief. Immortality doesn't come with a long memory, thank god. I can forget most of it.

Just have to give it time. Hopefully Brandon won't forget quickly.

About the Author

Caitlin is a cat lover, writer, amateur chef and wicked great at trivia. She likes drinking wine and playing D&D, especially simultaneously. Her love of mythology began at a very young age, and she still dreams of visiting Greece one day to see the source of these ancient stories.

Even though she doesn't like beer, Caitlin loves living in Kalamazoo and visiting the local breweries. She believes in supporting small business and independent artists, and hopes to encourage others to do so as well.

Also from Arctos Media

Vengeance is a Wheel by Clifford VanMeter

H-Investigations by Caitlin VanMeter

The Spiral Arm Stories by Clifford VanMeter

**Learn more at
CliffordVanMeter.com
CaitlinVanMeter.com**